The Star Hyacinths

Other Books by James H. Schmitz

The Demon Breed
The Universe Against Her
The Witches of Karres

The Star Hyacinths

James H. Schmitz

ÆGYPAN PRESS

This text from *Amazing Stories*, December, 1961.

Special thanks to Greg Weeks, Stephen Blundell, and
the Online Distributed Proofreading Team (which can
be found at http://www.pgdp.net).

The Star Hyacinths
A publication of
ÆGYPAN PRESS
www.aegypan.com

On a bleak, distant uncharted world two ships lay wrecked and a lone man stared at a star hyacinth. Its brilliance burned into his retina . . . and he knew that men could easily kill and kill for that one beauty alone.

*T*he robbery of the Dosey Asteroids Shipping Station in a remote and spottily explored section of space provided the newscasting systems of the Federation of the Hub with one of the juiciest crime stories of the season. In a manner not clearly explained, the Dosey Asteroids Company had lost six months' production of gem-quality cut star hyacinths valued at nearly a hundred million credits. It lost also its Chief Lapidary and seventy-eight other company employees who had been in the station dome at the time.

All these people appeared at first to have been killed by gunfire, but a study of their bodies revealed that only in a few instances had gun wounds been the actual cause of death. For the most part the wounds had been inflicted on corpses, presumably in an attempt to conceal the fact that disaster in another and unknown form had befallen the station.

The raiders left very few clues. It appeared that the attack on the station had been carried out by a single ship, and that the locks to the dome had been opened from within. The latter fact, of course, aroused speculation, but led the investigators nowhere.

Six years later the great Dosey Asteroids robbery remained an unsolved mystery.

*T*he two wrecked spaceships rested almost side by side near the tip of a narrow, deep arm of a great lake.

The only man on the planet sat on a rocky ledge three miles uphill from the two ships, gazing broodingly down at them. He was a big fellow in neatly patched shipboard clothing. His hands were clean, his face carefully shaved. He had two of the castaway's traditional possessions with him; a massive hunting bow rested against the rocks, and a minor representative of the class of life which was this world's equivalent of birds was hopping about near his feet. This was a thrush-sized creature with a jaunty bearing and bright yellow eyes. From the front of its round face protruded a short, narrow tube tipped with small, sharp teeth. Round, horny knobs at the ends of its long toes protected retractile claws as it bounded back and forth between the bow and the man, giving a quick flutter of its wings on each bound. Finally it stopped before the man, stretching its neck to stare up at him, trying to catch his attention.

He roused from his musing, glanced irritably down at it.

"Not now, Birdie," he said. "Keep quiet!"

The man's gaze returned to the two ships, then passed briefly along a towering range of volcanoes on the other side of the lake, and lifted to the cloudless blue sky. His eyes probed on, searching the sunlit, empty vault above him. If a ship ever came again, it would come from there, the two wrecks by the lake arm already fixed in its detectors; it would not come gliding along the surface of the planet. . . .

Birdie produced a sharp, plaintive whistle. The man looked at it.

"Shut up, stupid!" he told it.

He reached into the inner pocket of his coat, took out a small object wrapped in a piece of leather, and unfolded the leather.

Then it lay in his cupped palm, and blazed with the brilliance of twenty diamonds, seeming to flash the fires of the spectrum furiously from every faceted surface, without ever quite subduing the pure violet luminance which made a star hyacinth impossible to imitate or, once seen, to forget. The most beautiful of gems, the rarest, the most valuable. The man who was a castaway stared at it for long seconds, his breath quickening and his hand beginning to tremble. Finally he folded the chip of incredible mineral back into the leather, replaced it carefully in his pocket.

When he looked about again, the sunlit air seemed brighter, the coloring of lake and land more vivid and alive. Once during each of this world's short days, but no oftener, he permitted himself to look at the star hyacinth. It was a ritual adhered to with almost religious strictness, and it had kept him as sane as he was ever likely to be again, for over six years.

It might, he sometimes thought, keep him sane until a third ship presently came along to this place. And then . . .

The third ship was coming along at the moment, still some five hours' flight out from the system. She was a small ship with lean, rakish lines, a hot little speedster, gliding placidly through subspace just now, her engines throttled down.

Aboard her, things were less peaceful.

*T*he girl was putting up a pretty good fight but getting nowhere with it against the bull-necked Fleetman who had her pinned back against the wall.

Wellan Dasinger paused in momentary indecision at the entrance to the half-darkened control section of the speedboat. The scuffle in there very probably was none of his business. The people of the roving Independent Fleets had their own practices and mores and resented interference from uninformed planet dwellers. For all Dasinger knew, their blue-eyed lady pilot enjoyed roughhousing with the burly members of her crew. If the thing wasn't serious. . . .

He heard the man rap out something in the Willata Fleet tongue, following the words up with a solid thump of his fist into the girl's side. The thump hadn't been playful, and her sharp gasp of pain indicated no enjoyment whatever. Dasinger stepped quickly into the room.

He saw the girl turn startled eyes toward him as he came up behind the man. The man was Liu Taunus, the bigger of the two crew members . . . too big and too well muscled by a good deal, in fact, to make a sportsmanlike suggestion to divert his thumpings to Dasinger look like a sensible approach. Besides Dasinger didn't know the Willata Fleet's language. The edge of his hand slashed twice from behind along the thick neck; then his fist brought the breath whistling from Taunus's lungs before the Fleetman had time to turn fully towards him.

It gave Dasinger a considerable starting advantage. During the next twenty seconds or so the advantage seemed to diminish rapidly. Taunus's fists and boots had scored only near misses so far, but he began to look like the hardest big man to chop down Dasinger had yet run into. And then the Fleetman was suddenly sprawling on the floor, face down, arms flung out limply, a tough boy with a thoroughly bludgeoned nervous system.

Dasinger was straightening up when he heard the *thunk* of the wrench. He turned sharply, discovered first the girl standing ten feet away with the wrench in her raised hand, next their second crew member lying on the carpet between them, finally the long, thin knife lying near the man's hand.

"Thanks, Miss Mines!" he said, somewhat out of breath. "I really should have remembered Calat might be somewhere around."

Duomart Mines gestured with her head at the adjoining control cabin. "He was in there," she said, also breathlessly. She was a long-legged blonde with a limber way of moving, pleasing to look at in her shaped Fleet uniform, though with somewhat aloof and calculating eyes. In the dim light of the room she seemed to be studying Dasinger now with an expression somewhere between wariness and surprised speculation. Then, as he took a step forward to check on Calat's condition, she backed off slightly, half lifting the wrench again.

Dasinger stopped and looked at her. "Well," he said, "make up your mind! Whose side are you on here?"

Miss Mines hesitated, let the wrench down. "Yours, I guess," she acknowledged. "I'd better be, now! They'd murder me for helping a planeteer."

*D*asinger went down on one knee beside Calat, rather cautiously though the Fleetman wasn't stirring, and picked up the knife. Miss Mines turned up the room's lights. Dasinger asked, "What was this . . . a mutiny? You're technically in charge of the ship, aren't you?"

"Technically," she agreed, added, "We were arguing about a Fleet matter."

"I see. We'll call it mutiny." Dasinger checked to be sure Calat wasn't faking unconsciousness. He inquired, "Do you really need these boys to help you?"

Duomart Mines shook her blond head. "Not at all. Flying the Mooncat is a one-man job."

"I did have a feeling," Dasinger admitted, "that Willata's Fleet was doing a little feather-bedding when they said I'd have to hire a crew of three to go along with their speedboat."

"Uh-huh." Her tone was non-committal. "They were. What are you going to do with them?"

"Anywhere they can be locked up safely?"

"Not safely. Their own cabin's as good as anything. They can batter their way out of here if they try hard enough. Of course we'd hear them doing it."

"Well, we can fix that." Dasinger stood up, fished his cabin key out of a pocket and gave it to her. "Tan suitcase standing at the head of my bunk," he said. "Mind bringing that and the little crane from the storeroom up here?"

Neither of the Fleetmen had begun to stir when Duomart Mines came riding a gravity crane back in through the door a couple of minutes later, the suitcase dangling in front of her. She halted the crane in the center of the room, slid out of its saddle with a supple twist of her body, and handed Dasinger his cabin key.

"Thanks." Dasinger took the suitcase from the crane, unlocked and opened it. He brought out a pair of plastic handcuffs, aware that Miss Mines stood behind him making an intent scrutiny of what could be seen of the suitcase's contents. He didn't blame her for feeling curious; she was looking at a variety of devices which might have delighted the eyes of both a professional burglar and military spy. She offered no comment.

Neither did Dasinger. He hauled Liu Taunus over on his back, fastened handcuffs about the Fleetman's wrists, then rolled him over on his face again. He did the same for Calat, hung the suitcase back in the crane, slung a leg across the crane's saddle and settled into it.

Miss Mines remarked, "I'd look their cabin over pretty closely for guns and so on before leaving them there."

"I intend to. By the way, has Dr. Egavine mentioned how close we are to our destination?" Dasinger maneuvered the crane over to Taunus, lowered a beam to the small of the Fleetman's back and hoisted him up carefully, arms, head and legs dangling.

The blond girl checked her watch. "He didn't tell me exactly," she said, "but there's what seems to be a terraprox in the G2 system ahead. If that's it, we'll get there in around five hours depending on what subspace conditions in the system are. Dr. Egavine's due up here in thirty minutes to give me the final figures." She paused, added curiously, "Don't you know yourself just where we're going?"

"No," Dasinger said. "I'm financing the trip. The doctor is the man with the maps and other pertinent information."

"I thought you were partners."

"We are. Dr. Egavine is taciturn about some things. I'll bring him back here with me as soon as I have these two locked away." Dasinger finished picking up Calat, swung the crane slowly towards the door, the unconscious Fleet-men suspended ahead of him.

Dr. Egavine stood at the open door to his stateroom as Dasinger came walking back up the passage from the crew quarters and the storage. Quist, the doctor's manservant, peered out of the stateroom behind him.

"What in heaven's name were you doing with those two men?" Egavine inquired, twitching his eyebrows disapprovingly up and down. The doctor was a tall, thin man in his forties, dressed habitually in undertaker black, with bony features and intense dark eyes. He added, "They appeared to be unconscious . . . and fettered!"

"They were both," Dasinger admitted. "I've confined them to their cabin."

"Why?"

"We had a little slugfest in the control section a few minutes ago. One of the boys was beating around on our pilot, so I laid him out, and she laid out the other one when he tried to get into the act with a knife. She says the original dispute was a Fleet matter . . . in other words, none of our business. However, I don't know. There's something decidedly fishy about the situation."

"In what way?" Egavine asked.

Dasinger said, "I checked over the crew quarters for weapons just now and found something which suggests that Willata's Fleet is much more interested in what we're doing out here than we thought."

Egavine looked startled, peered quickly along the passage to the control section. "I feel," he said, lowering his voice, "that we should continue this discussion behind closed doors. . . ."

"All right." Quist, a bandy-legged, wiry little man with a large bulb of a nose and close-set, small eyes, moved back from the door. Dasinger went inside. Egavine pulled the door shut behind them and drew a chair out from the cabin table. Dasinger sat down opposite him.

"What did you find?" Dr. Egavine asked.

Dasinger said, "You know Miss Mines is supposed to be the only Fleet member on board who speaks the Federation's translingue. However, there was a listening device attached to the inside of the cabin communicator in the crew quarters. Its settings show that the Willata Fleet people have bugged each of the Mooncat's other cabins, and also — which I think is an interesting point — the control section. Have you and Quist discussed our project in any detail since coming aboard?"

"I believe we did, on several occasions," Egavine said hesitantly.

"Then we'd better assume Taunus and Calat knew that we're looking for the wreck of the Dosey Asteroids raider, and . . ."

Egavine put a cautioning finger to his lips. "Should we. . .?"

"Oh, no harm in talking now," Dasinger assured him. "I pulled the instrument out and dropped it in my cabin. Actually, the thing needn't be too serious if we stay on guard. But of course we shouldn't go back to the Fleet station after we have the stuff. Gadgetry of that kind suggests bad intentions . . . also a rather sophisticated level of criminality for an I-Fleet. We'll return directly to the Hub. We might have to go on short rations for a few weeks, but we'll make it. And we'll keep those two so-called crew members locked up."

The doctor cleared his throat. "Miss Mines . . ."

"She doesn't appear to be personally in-volved in any piratical schemes," Dasinger said. "Otherwise they wouldn't have bugged her cabin and the control rooms. If we dangle a few star hyacinths before her eyes, she should be willing to fly us back. If she balks, I think I can handle the Mooncat well enough to get us there."

Dr. Egavine tugged pensively at his ear lobe. "I see." His hand moved on toward his right coat lapel. "What do you think of . . ."

"Mind watching this for a moment, doctor?" Dasinger interrupted. He nodded at his own hand lying on the table before him.

"Watch. . .?" Egavine began questioningly. Then his eyes went wide with alarm.

Dasinger's hand had turned suddenly sideways from the wrist, turned up again. There was a small gun in the hand now, its stubby muzzle pointing up steadily at Egavine's chest.

"Dasinger! What does . . ."

"Neat trick, eh?" Dasinger commented. "Sleeve gun. Now keep quiet and hold everything just as it is. If you move or Quist over there moves before I tell you to, you've had it, doctor!"

*H*e reached across the table with his left hand, slipped it beneath Egavine's right coat lapel, tugged sharply at something in there, and brought out a flat black pouch with a tiny spray needle projecting from it. He dropped the pouch in his pocket, said, "Keep your seat, doctor," stood up and went over to Quist. Quist darted an anxious glance at his employer, and made a whimpering sound in his throat.

"You're not getting hurt," Dasinger told him. "Just put your hands on top of your head and stand still. Now let's take a look at the thing you started to pull from your pocket a moment ago . . . Electric stunsap, eh? That wasn't very nice of you, Quist! Let's see what else —

"Good Lord, Egavine," he announced presently, "your boy's a regular armory! Two blasters, a pencil-beam, a knife, and the sap . . . All right, Quist. Go over and sit down with the doctor." He watched the little man move deject-edly to the table, then fitted the assorted lethal devices carefully into one of his coat pockets, brought the pouch he had taken from Egavine out of the other pocket.

"Now, doctor," he said, "let's talk. I'm unhappy about this. I discovered you were car-rying this thing around before we left Mezmiali, and I had a sample of its contents analyzed. I was told it's a hypnotic with an almost instantaneous effect both at skin contact and when inhaled. Care to comment?"

"I do indeed!" Egavine said frigidly. "I have no intention of denying that the instrument is a hypnotic spray. As you know, I dislike guns and similar weapons, and we are engaged in a matter in which the need to defend myself against a personal attack might arise. Your assumption, however, that I intended to employ the spray on you just now is simply ridiculous!"

"I might be chuckling myself," Dasinger said, "if Quist hadn't had the sap halfway out of his pocket as soon as you reached for your lapel. If I'd ducked from the spray, I'd have backed into the sap, right? There's a little too much at stake here, doctor. You may be telling the truth, but just in case you're nourishing unfriendly ideas — and that's what it looks like to me — I'm taking a few precautions."

Dr. Egavine stared at him, his mouth set in a thin, bitter line. Then he asked, "What kind of precautions?"

Dasinger said, "I'll keep the hypnotic and Quist's bag of dirty tricks until we land. You might need those things on the planet but you don't need them on shipboard. You and I'll go up to the control section now to give Miss Mines her final flight directions. After that, you and Quist stay in this cabin with the door locked until the ship has set down. I don't want to have anything else to worry about while we're making the approach. If my suspicions turn out to be unjustified, I'll apologize . . . after we're all safely back in the Hub."

"What was your partner looking so sour about?" Duomart Mines inquired a little later, her eyes on the flight screens. "Have a quarrel with him?"

Dasinger, standing in the entry to the little control cabin across from her, shrugged his shoulders.

"Not exactly," he said. "Egavine tried to use a hypno spray on me."

"Hypno spray?" the young woman asked.

"A chemical which induces an instantaneous hypnotic trance in people. Leaves them wide open to suggestion. Medical hypnotists make a lot of use of it. So do criminals."

She turned away from the control console to look at him. "Why would your partner want to hypnotize you?"

"I don't know," Dasinger said. "He hasn't admitted that he intended to do it."

"Is he a criminal?"

"I wouldn't say he isn't," Dasinger observed judiciously, "but I couldn't prove it."

Duomart puckered her lips, staring at him thoughtfully. "What about yourself?" she asked.

"No, Miss Mines, I have a very high regard for the law. I'm a simple businessman."

"A simple businessman who flies his own cruiser four weeks out from the Hub into I-Fleet territory?"

"That's the kind of business I'm in," Dasinger explained. "I own a charter ship company."

"I see," she said. "Well, you two make an odd pair of partners. . . ."

"I suppose we do. Incidentally, has there been any occasion when you and Dr. Egavine — or you and Dr. Egavine and his servant — were alone somewhere in the ship together? For example, except when we came up here to give you further flight instructions, did he ever enter the control room?"

She shook her blond head. "No. Those are the only times I've seen him."

"Certain of that?" he asked.

Duomart nodded without hesitation. "Quite certain!"

Dasinger took an ointment tube from his pocket, removed its cap, squeezed a drop of black, oily substance out on a fingertip. "Mind rolling up your sleeve a moment?" he asked. "Just above the elbow. . . ."

"What for?"

"It's because of the way those hypno sprays work," Dasinger said. "Give your victim a dose of the stuff, tell him what to do, and it usually gets done. And if you're being illegal about it, one of the first things you tell him to do is to forget he's ever been sprayed. This goop is designed for the specific purpose of knocking out hypnotic commands. Just roll up your sleeve like a good girl now, and I'll rub a little of it on your arm."

"You're not rubbing anything on my arm, mister!" Duomart told him coldly.

Dasinger shrugged resignedly, recapped the tube, and dropped it in his pocket. "Have it your way then," he remarked. "I was only . . ."

He lunged suddenly towards her.

Duomart gave him quite a struggle. A minute or two later, he had her down on the floor, her body and one arm clamped between his knees, while he unzipped the cuff on the sleeve of the other arm and pulled the sleeve up. He brought out the tube of antihypno ointment and rubbed a few drops of the ointment into the hollow of Duomart's elbow, put the tube back in his pocket, then went on holding her down for nearly another minute. She was gasping for breath, blue eyes furious, muscles tensed.

*S*uddenly he felt her relax. An expression of stunned surprise appeared on her face. "Why," she began incredulously, "he *did* . . ."

"Gave you the spray treatment, eh?" Dasinger said, satisfied. "I was pretty sure he had."

"Why, that — At his beck and call, he says! Well, we'll just see about . . . let me up, Dasinger! Just wait till I get my hands on that bony partner of yours!"

"Now take it easy."

"Take it easy! Why should I? I . . ."

"It would be better," Dasinger explained, "if Egavine believes you're still under the influence."

She scowled up at him; then her face turned thoughtful. "Ho! You feel it isn't that he's a depraved old goat, that he's got something more sinister in mind?"

"It's a definite possibility. Why not wait and find out? The ointment will immunize you against further tricks."

Miss Mines regarded him consideringly for a few seconds, then nodded. "All right! You can let me up now. What do you think he's planning?"

"Not easy to say with Dr. Egavine. He's a devious man." Dasinger got himself disentangled, came to his feet, and reached down to help her scramble up.

"They certainly wrap you up with that hypno stuff, don't they!" she observed wonderingly.

Dasinger nodded. "They certainly do!" Then he added, "I'm keeping the doctor and his little sidekick locked up, too, until we get to the planet. That leaves you and me with the run of the ship."

Duomart looked at him. "So it does," she agreed.

"Know how to use a gun?"

"Of course. But I'm not allow — I don't have one with me on this trip."

*H*e reached into his coat, took out a small gun in a fabric holster. Duomart glanced at it, then her eyes went back to his face.

"Might clip it to your belt," Dasinger said. "It's a good little shocker, fifty-foot range, safe for shipboard use. It's got a full load, eighty shots. We may or may not run into emergencies. If we don't, you'll still be more comfortable carrying it."

Duomart holstered the gun and attached the holster to her belt. She slid the tip of her tongue reflectively out between her lips, drew it back, blinked at the flight screens for a few seconds, then looked across at Dasinger and tapped the holster at her side.

"That sort of changes things, too!" she said.

"Changes what?"

"Tell you in a minute. Sit down, Dasinger. Manual course corrections coming up. . . ." She slid into the pilot seat, moved her hands out over the controls, and appeared to forget about him.

Dasinger settled into a chair to her left, lit a cigarette, smoked and watched her, glancing occasionally at the screens. She was jockeying the Mooncat deftly in and out of the fringes of a gravitic stress knot, presently brought it into the clear, slapped over a direction lever and slid the palm of her right hand along a row of speed control buttons depressing them in turn.

"Nice piece of piloting," Dasinger observed.

Duomart lifted one shoulder in a slight shrug. "That's my job." Her face remained serious. "Are you wondering why I edged us through that thing instead of going around it?"

"Uh-huh, a little," Dasinger admitted.

"It knocked half an hour off the time it should take us to get to your planet," she said.

"That is, if you'll still want to go there. We're being followed, you see."

"By whom?"

"They call her the Spy. After the Mooncat she's the fastest job in the Fleet. She's got guns, and her normal complement is twenty armed men."

"The idea being to have us lead them to what we're after, and then take it away from us?" Dasinger asked.

"That's right. I'm not supposed to know about it. You know what a Grey Fleet is?"

Dasinger nodded. "An Independent that's turned criminal."

"Yes. Willata's Fleet was a legitimate outfit up to four years ago. Then Liu Taunus and Calat and their gang took over. That happened to be the two Fleet bosses you slapped handcuffs on, Dasinger. We're a Grey Fleet now. So I had some plans of my own for this trip. If I can get to some other I-Fleet or to the Hub, I might be able to do something about Taunus.

After we were down on the planet, I was going to steal the Mooncat and take off by myself."

"Why are you telling me?"

Miss Mines colored a little. "Well, you gave me the gun," she said. "And you clobbered Taunus, and got me out of that hypno thing . . . I mean, I'd have to be pretty much of a jerk to ditch you now, wouldn't I? Anyway, now that I've told you, you won't be going back to Willata's Fleet, whatever you do. I'll still get to the Hub." She paused. "So what do you want to do now? Beat it until the coast's clear, or make a quick try for your loot before the Spy gets there?"

"How far is she behind us?" Dasinger asked.

Duomart said, "I don't know exactly. Here's what happened. When we started out, Taunus told me not to let the Mooncat travel at more than three-quarters speed for any reason. I figured then the Spy was involved in whatever he was planning; she can keep up with us at that rate, and she has considerably better detector reach than the Cat. She's stayed far enough back not to register on our plates throughout the trip.

"Late yesterday we hit some extensive turbulence areas, and I started playing games. There was this little cluster of three sun systems ahead. One of them was our target, though Dr. Egavine hadn't yet said which. I ducked around a few twisters, doubled back, and there was the Spy coming the other way. I beat it then — top velocity. The Spy dropped off our detectors two hours later, and she can't have kept us on for more than another hour herself.

"So they'll assume we're headed for one of those three systems, but they don't know which one. They'll have to look for us. There's only one terraprox in the system we're going to. There may be none in the others, or maybe four or five. But the terraprox worlds is where they'll look because the salvage suits you're carrying are designed for ordinary underwater work. After the way I ran from them, they'll figure something's gone wrong with Taunus's plans, of course."

Dasinger rubbed his chin. "And if they're lucky and follow us straight in to the planet?"

"Then," Miss Mines said, "you might still have up to six or seven hours to locate the stuff you want, load it aboard and be gone again."

"Might have?"

She shrugged. "We've got a lead on them, but just how big a lead we finally wind up with depends to a considerable extent on the flight conditions they run into behind us. They might get a break there, too. Then there's another very unfortunate thing. The system Dr. Egavine's directed us to now is the one we were closest to when I broke out of detection range. They'll probably decide to look there first. You see?"

"Yes," Dasinger said. "Not so good, is it?" He knuckled his jaw again reflectively.

"Why was Taunus pounding around on you when I came forward?"

"Oh, those two runches caught me flying the ship at top speed. Taunus was furious. He couldn't know whether the Spy still had a fix on us or not. Of course he didn't tell me that. The lumps he was preparing to hand out were to be for disregarding his instructions. He does things like that." She paused. "Well, are you going to make a try for the planet?"

"Yes," Dasinger said. "If we wait, there's entirely too good a chance the Spy will run across what we're after while she's snooping around for us there. We'll try to arrange things for a quick getaway in case our luck doesn't hold up."

Duomart nodded. "Mind telling me what you're after?"

"Not at all. Under the circumstances you should be told. . . .

"Of course," Dasinger concluded a minute or two later, "all we'll have a legal claim to is the salvage fee."

Miss Mines glanced over at him, looking somewhat shaken. "You *are* playing this legally?"

"Definitely."

"Even so," she said, "if that really is the wreck of the Dosey Asteroids raider, and the stones are still on board . . . you two will collect something like ten million credits between you!"

"Roughly that," Dasinger agreed. "Dr. Egavine learned about the matter from one of your Willata Fleetmen."

Her eyes widened. "He what!"

"The Fleet lost a unit called Handing's Scout about four years ago, didn't it?"

"Three and a half," she said. She paused. "Handing's Scout is the other wreck down there?"

"Yes. There was one survivor . . . as far as we know. You may recall his name. Leed Farous."

Duomart nodded. "The little kwil hound. He was assistant navigator. How did Dr. Egavine. . .?"

Dasinger said, "Farous died in a Federation hospital on Mezmiali two years ago, apparently of the accumulative effects of kwil addiction. He'd been picked up in Hub space in a lifeboat which we now know was one of the two on Handing's Scout."

"In Hub space? Why, it must have taken him almost a year to get that far in one of those tubs!"

"From what Dr. Egavine learned," Dasinger said, "it did take that long. The lifeboat couldn't be identified at the time. Neither could Farous. He was completely addled with kwil . . . quite incoherent, in fact already apparently in the terminal stages of the addiction. Strenuous efforts were made to identify him because a single large star hyacinth had been found in the lifeboat . . . there was the possibility it was one of the stones the Dosey Asteroids Company had lost. But Farous died some months later without regaining his senses sufficiently to offer any information.

"Dr. Egavine was the physician in charge of the case, and eventually also the man who signed the death certificate. The doctor stayed on at the hospital for another year, then resigned, announcing that he intended to go into private research. Before Farous died, Egavine had of course obtained his story from him."

Miss Mines looked puzzled. "If Farous never regained his senses . . ."

"Dr. Egavine is a hypnotherapist of exceptional ability," Dasinger said. "Leed Farous wasn't so far gone that the information couldn't be pried out of him with an understanding use of drug hypnosis."

"Then why didn't others . . ."

"Oh, it was attempted. But you'll remember," Dasinger said, "that I had a little trouble getting close to you with an antihypnotic. The good doctor got to Farous first, that's all. Instead of the few minutes he spent on you, he could put in hour after hour conditioning Farous. Later comers simply didn't stand a chance of getting through to him."

*D*uomart Mines was silent a moment, then asked, "Why did you two come out to the Willata Fleet station and hire one of our ships? Your cruiser's a lot slower than the Mooncat but it would have got you here."

Dasinger said, "Dr. Egavine slipped up on one point. One can hardly blame him for it since interstellar navigation isn't in his line. The reference points on the maps he had Farous make up for him turned out to be meaningless when compared with Federation star charts. We needed the opportunity to check them against your Fleet maps. They make sense then."

"I see." Duomart gave him a sideways glance, remarked, "You know, the way you've put it, the thing's still pretty fishy."

"In what manner?"

"Dr. Egavine finished off old Farous, didn't he?"

"He may have," Dasinger conceded. "It would be impossible to prove it now. You can't force a man to testify against himself. It's true, of course, that Farous died at a very convenient moment, from Dr. Egavine's point of view."

"Well," she said, "a man like that wouldn't be satisfied with half a salvage fee when he saw the chance to quietly make away with the entire Dosey Asteroids haul."

"That could be," Dasinger said thoughtfully. "On the other hand, a man who had committed an unprovable murder to obtain a legal claim to six million credits might very well decide not to push his luck any farther. You know the space salvage ruling that when a criminal act or criminal intent can be shown in connection with an operation like this, the guilty person automatically forfeits any claim he has to the fee."

"Yes, I know . . . and of course," Miss Mines said, "you aren't necessarily so lily white either. That's another possibility. And there's still another one. You don't happen to be a Federation detective, do you?"

Dasinger blinked. After a moment he said, "Not a bad guess. However, I don't work for the Federation."

"Oh? For whom do you work?"

"At the moment, and indirectly, for the Dosey Asteroids Company."

"Insurance?"

"No. After Farous died, Dosey Asteroids employed a detective agency to investigate the matter. I represent the agency."

"The agency collects on the salvage?"

"That's the agreement. We deliver the goods or get nothing."

"And Dr. Egavine?"

Dasinger shrugged. "If the doctor keeps his nose clean, he stays entitled to half the salvage fee."

"What about the way he got the information from Farous?" she asked.

"From any professional viewpoint, that was highly unethical procedure. But there's no evidence Egavine broke any laws."

Miss Mines studied him, her eyes bright and quizzical. "I had a feeling about you," she said. "I . . ."

A warning burr came from the tolerance indicator; the girl turned her head quickly, said, "Cat's complaining . . . looks like we're hitting the first system stresses!" She slid back into the pilot seat. "Be with you again in a while. . . ."

When Dasinger returned presently to the control section Duomart sat at ease in the pilot seat with coffee and a sandwich before her.

"How are the mutineers doing?" she asked.

"They ate with a good appetite, said nothing, and gave me no trouble," Dasinger said. "They still pretend they don't understand

Federation translingue. Dr. Egavine's a bit sulky. He wanted to be up front during the prelanding period. I told him he could watch things through his cabin communicator screen."

Miss Mines finished her sandwich, her eyes thoughtful. "I've been wondering, you know . . . how can you be sure Dr. Egavine told you the truth about what he got from Leed Farous?"

Dasinger said, "I studied the recordings Dr. Egavine made of his sessions with Farous in the hospital. He may have held back on a few details, but the recordings were genuine enough."

"So Farous passes out on a kwil jag," she said, "and he doesn't even know they're making a landing. When he comes to, the scout's parked, the Number Three drive is smashed, the lock is open, and not another soul is aboard or in sight.

"Then he notices another wreck with its lock open, wanders over, sees a few bones and stuff lying around inside, picks up a star hyacinth, and learns from the ship's records that down in the hold under sixty feet of water is a sealed compartment with a whole little crateful of the stones. . . ."

"That's the story," Dasinger agreed.

"In the Fleets," she remarked, "if we heard of a place where a couple of ship's crews seemed to have vanished into thin air, we'd call it a spooked world. And usually we'd keep away from it." She clamped her lower lip lightly between her teeth for a moment. "Do you think Dr. Egavine has considered the kwil angle?"

Dasinger nodded. "I'm sure of it. Of course it's only a guess that the kwil made a difference for Farous. The stuff has no known medical value of any kind. But when the only known survivor of two crews happens to be a kwil-eater, the point has to be considered."

"Nobody else on Handing's Scout took kwil," Duomart said. "I know that. There aren't many in the Fleet who do." She hesitated. "You know, Dasinger, perhaps I should try it again! Maybe if I took it straight from the needle this time . . ."

Dasinger shook his head. "If the little flake you nibbled made you feel drowsy, even a quarter of a standard shot would put you out cold for an hour or two. Kwil has that effect on a lot of people. Which is one reason it isn't a very popular drug."

"What effect does it have on you?" she asked.

"Depends to some extent on the size of the dose. Sometimes it slows me down physically and mentally. At other times there were no effects that I could tell until the kwil wore off. Then I'd have hallucinations for a while — that can be very distracting, of course, when there's something you have to do. Those hangover hallucinations seem to be another fairly common reaction."

He concluded, "Since you can't take the drug and stay awake, you'll simply remain inside the locked ship. It will be better anyway to keep the Mooncat well up in the air and ready to move most of the time we're on the planet."

"What about Taunus and Calat?" she asked.

"They come out with us, of course. If kwil is what it takes to stay healthy down there, I've enough to go around. And if it knocks them out, it will keep them out of trouble."

*L*ooks like there's a firemaker down there!" Duomart's slim forefinger indicated a point on the ground-view plate. "Column of smoke starting to come up next to that big patch of trees!. . . Two point nine miles due north and uphill of the wrecks."

From a wall screen Dr. Egavine's voice repeated sharply, "Smoke? Then Leed Farous was not the only survivor!"

Duomart gave him a cool glance. "Might be a native animal that knows how to make fire. They're not so unusual." She went on to Dasinger. "It would take a hand detector to spot us where we are, but it does look like a distress signal. If it's men from one of the wrecks, why haven't they used the scout's other lifeboat?"

"Would the lifeboat still be intact?" Dasinger asked.

Duomart spun the ground-view plate back to the scout. "Look for yourself," she said. "It *couldn't* have been damaged in as light a crash as that one was. Those tubs are built to stand a really solid shaking up! And what else could have harmed it?"

"Farous may have put it out of commission before he left," Dasinger said. "He wanted to come back from the Hub with an expedition to get the hyacinths, so he wouldn't have cared for the idea of anyone else getting away from the planet meanwhile." He looked over at the screen. "How about it, doctor? Did Farous make any mention of that?"

Dr. Egavine seemed to hesitate an instant. "As a matter of fact, he did. Farous was approximately a third of the way to the Hub when he realized he might have made a mistake in not rendering the second lifeboat unusable. But by then it was too late to turn back, and of course he was almost certain there were no other survivors."

"So that lifeboat should still be in good condition?"

"It was in good condition when Farous left here."

"Well, whoever's down there simply may not know how to handle it."

Duomart shook her blond head decidedly. "That's out, too!" she said. "Our Fleet lifeboats all came off an old Grand Commerce liner which was up for scrap eighty, ninety years ago. They're designed so any fool can tell what to do, and the navigational settings are completely automatic. Of course if it *is* a native firemaker — with mighty keen eyesight — down there, that could be different! A creature like that mightn't think of going near the scout. Should I start easing the Cat in towards the smoke, Dasinger?"

"Yes. We'll have to find out what the signal means before we try to approach the wrecks. Doctor, are you satisfied now that Miss Mines's outworld biotic check was correct?"

"The analysis appears to be fairly accurate," Dr. Egavine acknowledged, "and all detectable trouble sources are covered by the selected Fleet serum."

*D*asinger said, "We'll prepare for an immediate landing then. There'll be less than an hour of daylight left on the ground, but the night's so short we'll disregard that factor." He switched off the connection to Egavine's cabin, turned to Duomart. "Now our wrist communicators, you say, have a five-mile range?"

"A little over five."

"Then," Dasinger said, "we'll keep you and the Cat stationed at an exact five-mile altitude ninety-five percent of the time we spend on the planet. If the Spy arrives while you're up there, how much time will we have to clear out?"

She shrugged. "That depends of course on how they arrive. My detectors can pick the

Spy up in space before their detectors can make out the Cat against the planet. If we spot them as they're heading in, we'll have around fifteen minutes.

"But if they show up on the horizon in atmosphere, or surface her out of subspace, that's something else. If I don't move instantly then, they'll have me bracketed . . . and BLOOIE!"

Dasinger said, "Then those are the possibilities you'll have to watch for. Think you could draw the Spy far enough away in a chase to be able to come back for us?"

"They wouldn't follow me that far," Duomart said. "They know the Cat can outrun them easily once she's really stretched out, so if they can't nail her in the first few minutes they'll come back to look around for what we were interested in here." She added, "And if I *don't* let the Cat go all out but just keep a little ahead of them, they'll know that I'm trying to draw them away from something."

Dasinger nodded. "In that case we'll each be on our own, and your job will be to keep right on going and get the information as quickly as possible to the Kyth detective agency in Orado. The agency will take the matter from there."

Miss Mines looked at him. "Aren't you sort of likely to be dead before the agency can do anything about the situation?"

"I'll try to avoid it," Dasinger said. "Now, we've assumed the worst as far as the Spy is concerned. But things might also go wrong downstairs. Say I lose control of the group, or we all get hit down there by whatever hit the previous landing parties and it turns out that kwil's no good for it. It's understood that in any such event you again head the Cat immediately for the Hub and get the word to the agency. Right?"

Duomart nodded.

He brought a flat case of medical hypodermics out of his pocket, and opened it.

"Going to take your shot of kwil before we land?" Miss Mines asked.

"No. I want you to keep one of these needles on hand, at least until we find out what the problem is. It'll knock you out if you have to take it, but it might also keep you alive. I'm waiting myself to see if it's necessary to go on kwil. The hallucinations I get from the stuff afterwards could hit me while we're in the middle of some critical activity or other, and that mightn't be so good." He closed the case again, put it away. "I think we've covered everything. If you'll check the view plate, something — or somebody — has come out from under the trees near the column of smoke. And unless I'm mistaken it's a human being."

Duomart slipped the kwil needle he'd given her into a drawer of the instrument console. "I don't think you're mistaken," she said. "I've been watching him for the last thirty seconds."

"It is a man?"

"Pretty sure of it. He moves like one."

Dasinger stood up. "I'll go talk with Egavine then. I had a job in mind for him and his hypno sprays if we happened to run into human survivors."

"Shall I put the ship down next to this one?"

"No. Land around five hundred yards to the north, in the middle of that big stretch of open ground. That should keep us out of ambushes. Better keep clear of the airspace immediately around the wrecks as you go down."

Duomart looked at him. "Darn right I'll keep clear of that area!"

Dasinger grinned. "Something about the scout?"

"Sure. No visible reason at all why the scout should have settled hard enough to buckle a drive. Handing was a good pilot."

"Hm-m-m." Dasinger rubbed his chin. "Well, I've been wondering. The Dosey Asteroids raiders are supposed to have used an unknown type of antipersonnel weapon in their attack on the station, you know. Nothing in sight on their wreck that might be, say, an automatic gun but . . . well, just move in carefully and stay ready to haul away very fast at the first hint of trouble!"

*T*he Mooncat slid slowly down through the air near the point where the man stood in open ground, a hundred yards from the clump of trees out of which smoke still billowed thickly upwards. The man watched the speedboat's descent quietly, making no further attempt to attract the attention of those on board to himself.

Duomart had said that the man was not a member of Handing's lost crew but a stranger. He was therefore one of the Dosey Asteroids raiders.

Putting down her two land legs, the Mooncat touched the open hillside a little over a quarter of a mile from the woods, stood straddled and rakish, nose high. The storeroom lock opened, and a slender ramp slid out. Quist showed in the lock, dumped two portable shelters to the ground, came scrambling nimbly down the ramp. Dr. Egavine followed, more cautiously, the two handcuffed Fleetmen behind him. Dasinger came out last, glancing over at the castaway who had started across the slope towards the ship.

"Everyone's out," he told his wrist communicator. "Take her up."

The ramp snaked soundlessly back into the lock, the lock snapped shut and the Mooncat lifted smoothly and quickly from the ground. Liu Taunus glanced after the rising speedboat, looked at Calat, and spoke loudly and emphatically in Fleetlingue for a few seconds, his broad face without expression. Dasinger said, "All right, Quist, break out the shelter."

When the shelter was assembled, Dasinger motioned the Fleetmen towards the door with his thumb. "Inside, boys!" he said. "Quist, lock the shelter behind them and stay on guard here. Come on, doctor. We'll meet our friend halfway. . . ."

*T*he castaway approached unhurriedly, walking with a long, easy stride, the bird thing on his shoulder craning its neck to peer at the strangers with round yellow eyes. The man was big and rangy, probably less heavy by thirty pounds than Liu Taunus, but in perfect physical condition. The face was strong and intelligent, smiling elatedly now.

"I'd nearly stopped hoping this day would arrive!" he said in translingue. "May I ask who you are?"

"An exploration group." Dasinger gripped the extended hand, shook it, as Dr. Egavine's right hand went casually to his coat lapel. "We noticed the two wrecked ships down by the lake," Dasinger explained, "then saw your smoke signal. Your name?"

"Graylock. Once chief engineer of the Antares, out of Vanadia on Aruaque." Graylock turned, still smiling, towards Egavine.

Egavine smiled as pleasantly.

"Graylock," he observed, "you feel, and will continue to feel, that this is the conversation you planned to conduct with us, that everything is going exactly in accordance with your wishes." He turned his head to Dasinger, inquired, "Would you prefer to question him yourself, Dasinger?"

Dasinger hesitated, startled; but Graylock's expression did not change. Dasinger shook his head. "Very smooth, doctor!" he commented. "No, go ahead. You're obviously the expert here."

"Very well . . . Graylock," Dr. Egavine resumed, "you will cooperate with me fully and to the best of your ability now, knowing that I am both your master and friend. Are any of the other men who came here on those two ships down by the water still alive?"

There was complete stillness for a second or two. Then Graylock's face began to work unpleasantly, all color draining from it. He said harshly, "No. But I . . . I don't . . ." He stammered incomprehensibly, went silent again, his expression wooden and set.

"Graylock," Egavine continued to probe, "you can remember everything now, and you are not afraid. Tell me what happened to the other men."

Sweat covered the castaway's ashen face. His mouth twisted in agonized, silent grimaces again. The bird thing leaped from his shoulder with a small purring sound, fluttered softly away.

Dr. Egavine repeated, "You are not afraid. You can remember. What happened to them? How did they die?"

And abruptly the big man's face smoothed out. He looked from Egavine to Dasinger and back with an air of brief puzzlement, then explained conversationally, "Why, Hovig's generator killed many of us as we ran away from the Antares. Some reached the edges of the circle with me, and I killed them later."

Dr. Egavine flicked another glance towards Dasinger but did not pause.

"And the crew of the second ship?" he asked.

"Those two. They had things I needed, and naturally I didn't want them alive here."

"Is Hovig's generator still on the Antares?"

"Yes."

"How does the generator kill?"

Sweat suddenly started out on Graylock's face again, but now he seemed unaware of any accompanying emotions. He said, "It kills by fear, of course. . . ."

*T*he story of the Dosey Asteroids raider and of Hovig's fear generators unfolded quickly from there. Hovig had developed his machines for the single purpose of robbing the Dosey Asteroids Shipping Station. The plan then had been to have the Antares cruise in uncharted space with the looted star hyacinths for at least two years, finally to approach the area of the Federation from a sector far removed from the Dosey system. That precaution resulted in disaster for Hovig. Chief Engineer Graylock had time to consider that his share in the profits of the raid would be relatively insignificant, and that there was a possibility of increasing it.

Graylock and his friends attacked their shipmates as the raider was touching down to the surface of an uncharted world to replenish its water supply. The attack succeeded but Hovig, fatally wounded, took a terrible revenge on the mutineers. He contrived to set off one of his grisly devices, and to all intents and purposes everyone still alive on board the Antares immediately went insane with fear. The ship crashed out of control at the edge of a lake. Somebody had opened a lock and a number of the frantic crew plunged from the ramp and fell to their death on the rocks below. Those who reached the foot of the ramp fled frenziedly from the wreck, the effects of Hovig's machine pursuing them but weakening gradually as they widened the distance between themselves and the Antares. Finally, almost three miles away, the fear impulses faded out completely. . . .

But thereafter the wreck was unapproachable. The fear generator did not run out of power, might not run out of power for years.

Dasinger said, "Doctor, let's hurry this up! Ask him why they weren't affected by their murder machines when they robbed Dosey Asteroids. Do the generators have a beam-operated shut-off, or what?"

Graylock listened to the question, said, "We had taken kwil. The effects were still very unpleasant, but they could be tolerated."

There was a pause of a few seconds. Dr. Egavine cleared his throat. "It appears, Dasinger," he remarked, "that we have failed to consider a very important clue!"

Dasinger nodded. "And an obvious one," he said dryly. "Keep it moving along, doctor.

How much kwil did they take? How long had they been taking it before the raid?"

Dr. Egavine glanced over at him, repeated the questions.

Graylock said Hovig had begun conditioning the crew to kwil a week or two before the Antares slipped out of Aruaque for the strike on the station. In each case the dosage had been built up gradually to the quantity the man in question required to remain immune to the generators. Individual variations had been wide and unpredictable.

Dasinger passed his tongue over his lips, nodded. "Ask him . . ."

*H*e checked himself at a soft, purring noise, a shadowy fluttering in the air. Graylock's animal flew past him, settled on its master's shoulder, turned to stare at Dasinger and Egavine. Dasinger looked at the yellow owl-eyes, the odd little tube of a mouth, continued to Egavine, "Ask him where the haul was stored in the ship."

Graylock confirmed Leed Farous's statement of what he had seen in the Antares's records. All but a few of the star hyacinths had been placed in a vaultlike compartment in the storage, and the compartment was sealed. Explosives would be required to open it. Hovig kept out half a dozen of the larger stones, perhaps as an antidote to boredom during the long voyage ahead. Graylock had found one of them just before Hovig's infernal instrument went into action.

"And where is that one now?" Dr. Egavine asked.

"I still have it."

"On your person?"

"Yes."

Dr. Egavine held out his hand, palm upward. "You no longer want it, Graylock. Give it to me."

Graylock looked bewildered; for a moment he appeared about to weep. Then he brought a knotted piece of leather from his pocket, unwrapped it, took out the gem and placed it in Egavine's hand. Egavine picked it up between thumb and forefinger of his other hand, held it out before him.

There was silence for some seconds while the star hyacinth burned in the evening air and the three men and the small winged animal stared at it. Then Dr. Egavine exhaled slowly.

"Ah, now!" he said, his voice a trifle unsteady. "Men might kill and kill for that one beauty alone, that is true!. . . Will you keep it for now, Dasinger? Or shall I?"

Dasinger looked at him thoughtfully.

"You keep it, doctor," he said.

"Dasinger," Dr. Egavine observed a few minutes later, "I have been thinking. . . ."

"Yes?"

"Graylock's attempted description of his experience indicates that the machine on the Antares does not actually broadcast the emotion of terror, as he believes. The picture presented is that of a mind in which both the

natural and the acquired barriers of compart-
mentalization are temporarily nullified, result-
ing in an explosion of compounded insanity to
an extent which would be inconceivable without
such an outside agent. As we saw in Graylock,
the condition is in fact impossible to describe
or imagine! A diabolical device. . . ."

He frowned. "Why the drug kwil coun-
teracts such an effect remains unclear. But since
we now know that it does, I may have a solution
to the problem confronting us."

Dasinger nodded. "Let's hear it."

"Have Miss Mines bring the ship down
immediately," Egavine instructed him. "There
is a definite probability that among my medical
supplies will be an effective substitute for kwil,
for this particular purpose. A few hours of
experimentation, and . . ."

"Doctor," Dasinger interrupted, "hold it
right there! So far there's been no real harm in
sparring around. But we're in a different situation now . . . we may be running out of time
very quickly. Let's quit playing games."

Dr. Egavine glanced sharply across at him. "What do you mean?"

"I mean that we both have kwil, of course. There's no reason to experiment. But the fact that we have it is no guarantee that we'll be able to get near that generator. Leed Farous's tissues were soaked with the drug. Graylock's outfit had weeks to determine how much each of them needed to be able to operate within range of the machines and stay sane. We're likely to have trouble enough without trying to jockey each other."

Dr. Egavine cleared his throat. "But I . . ."

Dasinger interrupted again. "Your reluctance to tell me everything you knew or had guessed is understandable. You had no more reason to trust me completely than I had to trust you. So before you say anything else I'd like you to look at these credentials. You're familiar with the Federation seal, I think."

Dr. Egavine took the proffered identification case, glanced at Dasinger again, then opened the case.

"So," he said presently. "You're a detective working for the Dosey Asteroids Company. . . ." His voice was even. "That alters the situation, of course. Why didn't you tell me this?"

"That should be obvious," Dasinger said. "If you're an honest man, the fact can make no difference. The company remains legally bound to pay out the salvage fee for the star hyacinths. They have no objection to that. What they didn't like was the possibility of having the gems stolen for the second time. If that's what you had in mind, you wouldn't, of course, have led an agent of the company here. In other words, doctor, in cooperating with me you're running no risk of being cheated out of your half of the salvage rights."

Dasinger patted the gun in his coat pocket. "And of course," he added, "if I happened to be a bandit in spite of the credentials, I'd be eliminating you from the partnership right now instead of talking to you! The fact that I'm not doing it should be a sufficient guarantee that I don't intend to do it."

Dr. Egavine nodded. "I'm aware of the point."

"Then let's get on with the salvage," Dasinger said. "For your further information, there's an armed Fleet ship hunting for us with piratical intentions, and the probability is that it will find us in a matter of hours. . . ."

*H*e described the situation briefly, concluded, "You've carried out your part of the contract by directing us here. You can, if you wish, minimize further personal risks by using the Fleet scout's lifeboat to get yourself and Quist off the planet, providing kwil will get you to the scout. Set a normspace course for Orado then, and we'll pick you up after we've finished the job."

Dr. Egavine shook his head. "Thank you, but I'm staying. It's in my interest to give you what assistance I can . . . and, as you've surmised, I do have a supply of kwil. What is your plan?"

"Getting Hovig's generator shut off is the first step," Dasinger said. "And since we don't know what dosage of the drug is required for each of us, we'd be asking for trouble by approaching the Antares in the ship. Miss Mines happens to be a kwil-sensitive, in any case. So it's going to take hiking, and I'll start down immediately now. Would Graylock and the Fleetmen obey hypnotic orders to the extent of helping out dependably in the salvage work?"

Egavine nodded. "There is no question of that."

"Then you might start conditioning them to the idea now. From the outer appearance of the Antares, it may be a real job to cut through inside her to get to the star hyacinths. We have the three salvage suits. If I can make it to the generator, shut it off, and it turns out then that I need some hypnotized brawn down there, Miss Mines will fly over the shelter as a signal to start marching the men down."

"Why march? At that point, Miss Mines could take us to the wreck within seconds."

Dasinger shook his head. "Sorry, doctor. Nobody but Miss Mines or myself goes aboard the Mooncat until we either wind up the job or are forced to clear out and run. I'm afraid that's one precaution I'll have to take. When you get to the Antares we'll give each of the boys a full shot of kwil. The ones that don't go limp on it can start helping."

Dr. Egavine said reflectively, "You feel the drug would still be a requirement?"

"Well," Dasinger said, "Hovig appears to have been a man who took precautions, too. We know he had three generators and that he set off one of them. The question is where the other two are. It wouldn't be so very surprising, would it, if one or both of them turned out to be waiting for intruders in the vault where he sealed away the loot?"

*T*he night was cool. Wind rustled in the ground vegetation and the occasional patches of trees. Otherwise the slopes were quiet. The sky was covered with cloud layers through which the Mooncat drifted invisibly. In the infrared glasses Dasinger had slipped on when he started, the rocky hillside showed clear for two hundred yards, tinted green as though bathed by a strange moonlight; beyond was murky darkness.

"Still all right?" Duomart's voice inquired from the wrist communicator.

"Uh-huh!" Dasinger said. "A little nervous, but I'd be feeling that way in any case, under the circumstances."

"I'm not so sure," she said. "You've gone past the two and a half mile line from the generator. From what that Graylock monster said, you should have started to pick up its effects. Why not take your shot, and play safe?"

"No," Dasinger said. "If I wait until I feel something that can be definitely attributed to the machine, I can keep the kwil dose down to what I need. I don't want to load myself up with the drug anymore than I have to."

A stand of tall trees with furry trunks moved presently into range of the glasses, thick undergrowth beneath. Dasinger picked his way through the thickets with some caution. The indications so far had been that local animals had as much good reason to avoid the vicinity of Hovig's machine as human beings, but if there was any poisonous vermin in the area this would be a good place for it to be lurking. Which seemed a fairly reasonable apprehension. Other, equally definite, apprehensions looked less reasonable when considered objectively. If he stumbled on a stone, it produced a surge of sharp alarm which lingered for seconds; and his breathing had quickened much more than could be accounted for by the exertions of the downhill climb.

*F*ive minutes beyond the wood Dasinger emerged from the mouth of a narrow gorge, and stopped short with a startled exclamation. His hand dug hurriedly into his pocket for the case of kwil needles.

"What's the matter?" Duomart inquired sharply.

Dasinger produced a somewhat breathless laugh. "I've decided to take the kwil. At once!"

"You're feeling . . . things?" Her voice was also shaky.

"I'll say! Not just a matter of feeling it, either. For example, a couple of old friends are walking towards me at the moment. Dead ones, as it happens."

"Ugh!" she said faintly. "Hurry up!"

Dasinger shoved the needle's plunger a quarter of the way down on the kwil solution, pulled the needle out of his arm. He stood still for some seconds, filled his lungs with the cool night air, let it out in a long sigh.

"That did it!" he announced, his voice steadying again. "The stuff works fast. A quarter shot. . . ."

"Why did you wait so long?"

"It wasn't too bad till just now. Then suddenly . . . that generator can't be putting out evenly! Anyway, it hit me like a rock. I doubt you'd be interested in details."

"I wouldn't," Duomart agreed. "I'm crawly enough as it is up here. I wish we were through with this!"

"With just a little luck we should be off the planet in an hour."

By the time he could hear the lapping of the lake water on the wind, he was aware of the growing pulse of Hovig's generator ahead of him, alive and malignant in the night. Then the Fleet scout came into the glasses, a squat, dark ship, its base concealed in the growth that had sprung up around it after it piled up on the slope. Dasinger moved past the scout, pushing through bushy aromatic shrubbery which thickened as he neared the water. He felt physically sick and sluggish now, was aware, too, of an increasing reluctance to go on. He would need more of the drug before attempting to enter the Antares.

To the west, the sky was partly clear, and presently he saw the wreck of the Dosey Asteroids raider loom up over the edge of the lake arm, blotting out a section of stars. Still beyond the field of the glasses, it looked like an armored water animal about to crawl up on the slopes. Dasinger approached slowly, in foggy unwillingness, emerged from the bushes into open ground, and saw a broad ramp furred with a thick coat of moldlike growth rise steeply towards an open lock in the upper part of the Antares. The pulse of the generator might have been the beating of the maimed ship's heart, angry and threatening. It seemed to be growing stronger. And had something moved in the lock? Dasinger stood, senses swimming sickly, dreaming that something huge rose slowly, towered over him like a giant wave, leaned forwards. . . .

"Still all right?" Duomart inquired.

The wave broke.

"Dasinger! What's happened?"

"Nothing," Dasinger said, his voice raw. He pulled the empty needle out of his arm, dropped it. "But something nearly did! The kwil I took wasn't enough. I was standing here waiting to let that damned machine swamp me when you spoke."

"You should have heard what you sounded like over the communicator! I thought you were . . ." her voice stopped for an instant, began again. "Anyway," she said briskly, "you're loaded with kwil now, I hope?"

"More than I should be, probably." Dasinger rubbed both hands slowly down along his face. "Well, it couldn't be helped. That was pretty close, I guess! I don't even remember getting the hypo out of the case."

He looked back up at the looming bow of the Antares, unbeautiful enough but prosaically devoid of menace and mystery now, though the pulsing beat still came from there. A mechanical obstacle and nothing else. "I'm going on in now."

From the darkness within the lock came the smell of stagnant water, of old decay. The mold that proliferated over the ramp did not extend into the wreck. But other things grew inside, pale and oily tendrils festooning the walls. Dasinger removed his night glasses, brought out a pencil light, let the beam fan out, and moved through the lock.

The crash which had crumpled the ship's lower shell had thrust up the flooring of the lock compartment, turned it into what was nearly level footing now. On the right, a twenty-foot black gap showed between the ragged edge of the deck and the far bulkhead from which it had been torn. The oily plant life spread over the edges of the flooring and on down into the flooded lower sections of the Antares. The pulse of Hovig's generator came from above and the left where a passage slanted steeply up into the ship's nose. Dasinger turned towards the passage, began clambering up.

There was no guesswork involved in determining which of the doors along the passage hid the machine in what, if Graylock's story was correct, had been Hovig's personal stateroom. As Dasinger approached that point, it was like climbing into silent thunder. The door was locked, and though the walls beside it were warped and cracked, the cracks were too narrow to permit entry. Dasinger dug out a tool which had once been the prized property of one of Orado's more eminent safecrackers, and went to work on the lock. A minute or two later he forced the door partly back in its tilted frame, scrambled through into the cabin.

Not enough was left of Hovig after this span of time to be particularly offensive. The generator lay in a lower corner, half buried under other molded and unrecognizable debris. Dasinger uncovered it, feeling as if he were drowning in the invisible torrent pouring out from it, knelt down and placed the light against the wall beside him.

The machine matched Graylock's description. A pancake-shaped heavy plastic casing eighteen inches across, two thick studs set into its edge, one stud depressed and flush with the surface, the other extended. Dasinger thumbed experimentally at the extended stud, found it apparently immovable, took out his gun.

"How is it going, Dasinger?" Miss Mines asked.

"All right," Dasinger said. He realized he was speaking with difficulty. "I've found the thing! Trying to get it shut off now. Tell you in a minute. . . ."

He tapped the extended stud twice with the butt of the gun, then slashed heavily down. The stud flattened back into the machine. Its counterpart didn't move. The drowning sensations continued.

Dasinger licked his lips, dropped the gun into his pocket, brought out the lock opener. He had the generator's cover plate pried partway back when it shattered. With that, the thunder that wasn't sound ebbed swiftly from the cabin. Dasinger reached into the generator, wrenched out a power battery, snapping half a dozen leads.

He sat back on his heels, momentarily dizzy with relief, then climbed to his feet with the smashed components of Hovig's machine, and turned to the door. Something in the debris along the wall flashed dazzlingly in the beam of his light.

Dasinger stared at the star hyacinth for an instant, then picked it up. It was slightly larger than the one Graylock had carried out of the Antares with him, perfectly cut. He found four others of similar quality within the next minute, started back down to the lock compartment with what might amount to two million credits in honest money, around half that in the

Hub's underworld gem trade, in one of his pockets.

"Yes?"

"Got the thing's teeth pulled now."

"Thank God! Coming right down. . . ."

The Mooncat was sliding in from the south as Dasinger stepped out on the head of the ramp. "Lock's open," Duomart's voice informed him. "I'll come aft and help."

*I*t took four trips with the gravity crane to transfer the salvage equipment into the Antares's lock compartment. Then Miss Mines sealed the Mooncat and went back upstairs. Dasinger climbed into one of the three salvage suits, hung the wrist communicator inside the helmet, snapped on the suit's lights and went over to the edge of the compartment deck. Black water reflected the lights thirty feet below. He checked the assortment of tools attached to his belt, nudged the suit's gravity cutoff to the right, energized magnetic pads on knees, boot tips and wrists, then fly-walked rapidly down a bulkhead and dropped into the water.

"No go, Duomart!" he informed the girl ten minutes later, his voice heavy with disappointment. "It's an ungodly twisted mess down here . . . worse than I thought it might be! Looks as if we'll have to cut all the way through to that vault. Give Egavine the signal to start herding the boys down."

Approximately an hour afterwards, Miss Mines reported urgently through the communicator, "They'll reach the lock in less than four minutes now, Dasinger! Better drop it and come up!"

"I'm on my way." Dasinger reluctantly switched off the beam-saw he was working with, fastened it to the belt of the salvage suit, turned in the murky water and started back towards the upper sections of the wreck. The job of getting through the tangled jungle of metal and plastic to the gem vault appeared no more than half completed, and the prospect of being delayed over it until the Spy discovered them here began to look like a disagreeably definite possibility. He clambered and floated hurriedly up through the almost vertical passage he'd cleared, found daylight flooding the lock compartment, the system's yellow sun well above the horizon. Peeling off the salvage suit, he restored the communicator to his wrist and went over to the head of the ramp.

*T*he five men came filing down the last slopes in the morning light, Taunus and Calat in the lead, Graylock behind them, the winged animal riding his shoulder and lifting occasionally into the air to flutter about the group. Quist and Egavine brought up the rear. Dasinger took the gun from his pocket.

"I'll clip my gun to the suit belt when I go back down in the water with the boys," he told the communicator. "If the doctor's turning any tricks over in his mind, that should give him food for thought. I'll relieve Quist of his weapon as he comes in."

"What about the guns in Graylock's hut?" Duomart asked.

"No charge left in them. If I'm reasonably careful, I really don't see what Dr. Egavine can do. He knows he loses his half-interest in the salvage the moment he pulls any illegal stunts."

A minute or two later, he called out, "Hold it there, doctor?"

The group shuffled to a stop near the foot of the ramp, staring up at him.

"Yes, Dasinger?" Dr. Egavine called back, sounding a trifle winded.

"Have Quist come up first and alone, please." Dasinger disarmed the little man at the entrance to the lock, motioned him on to the center of the compartment. The others arrived then in a line, filed past Dasinger and joined Quist.

"You've explained the situation to everybody?" Dasinger asked Egavine. There was an air of tenseness about the little group he didn't like, though tension might be understandable enough under the circumstances.

"Yes," Dr. Egavine said. "They feel entirely willing to assist us, of course." He smiled significantly.

"Fine." Dasinger nodded. "Line them up and let's get going! Taunus first. Get . . ."

There was a momentary stirring of the air back of his head. He turned sharply, jerking up the gun, felt twin needles drive into either side of his neck.

His body instantly went insensate. The lock appeared to circle about him, then he was on his back and Graylock's pet was alighting with a flutter of wings on his chest. It craned its head forward to peer into his face, the tip of its mouth tube open, showing a ring of tiny teeth. Vision and awareness left Dasinger together.

The other men hadn't moved. Now Dr. Egavine, his face a little pale, came over to Dasinger, the birdlike creature bounding back to the edge of the lock as he approached. Egavine knelt down, said quietly, his mouth near the wrist communicator, "Duomart Mines, you will obey me."

There was silence for a second or two. Then the communicator whispered, "Yes."

Dr. Egavine drew in a long, slow breath.

"You feel no question, no concern, no doubt about this situation," he went on. "You will bring the ship down now and land it safely beside the Antares. Then come up into the lock of the Antares for further instructions." Egavine stood up, his eyes bright with triumph.

*I*n the Mooncat three miles overhead, Duomart switched off her wrist communicator, sat white-faced, staring at the image of the Antares in the ground-view plate.

"Sweet Jana!" she whispered. "How did he . . . now what do I . . ."

She hesitated an instant, then opened a console drawer, took out the kwil needle Dasinger had left with her and slipped it into a pocket, clipped the holstered shocker back to her belt, and reached for the controls. A vast whistling shriek smote the Antares and the ears of those within as the Mooncat ripped down through atmosphere at an unatmospheric speed, leveled out smoothly and floated to the ground beside the wreck.

There was no one in sight in the lock of the Antares as Duomart came out and sealed the Mooncat's entry behind her. She went quickly up the broad, mold-covered ramp. The lock remained empty. From beyond it came the sound of some metallic object being pulled about, a murmur of voices. Twelve steps from the top, she took out the little gun, ran up to the lock and into it, bringing the gun up. She had a glimpse of Dr. Egavine and Quist stand-ing near a rusty bench in the compartment, of Graylock half into a salvage suit, Dasinger on the floor . . . then a flick of motion to right and left.

The tips of two space lines lashed about her simultaneously, one pinning her arms to her sides, the other clamping about her ankles and twitching her legs out from beneath her. She fired twice blindly to the left as the lines snapped her face down to the floor of the compartment. The gun was clamped beneath her stretched-out body and useless.

"What made that animal attack me anyway?" Dasinger asked wearily. He had just regained consciousness and been ordered by Calat to join the others on a rusted metal bench in the center of the lock compartment; Duomart to his left, Egavine on his right, Quist on the other side of Egavine. Calat stood watching them fifteen feet away, holding Dasinger's gun in one hand while he jiggled a few of Hovig's star hyacinths gently about in the other.

Calat's expression was cheerful, which made him the exception here. Liu Taunus and Graylock were down in the hold of the ship, working sturdily with cutter beams and power hoists to get to the sealed vault and blow it open.

How long they'd been at it, Dasinger didn't know.

"You can thank your double-crossing partner for what happened!" Duomart informed him. She looked pretty thoroughly mussed up though still unsubdued. "Graylock's been using the bird-thing to hunt with," she said. "It's a bloodsucker . . . nicks some animal with its claws and the animal stays knocked out while the little beast fills its tummy. So the intellectual over there had Graylock point you out to his pet, and it waited until your back was turned. . . ." She hesitated, went on less vehemently, "Sorry about not carrying out orders, Dasinger. I assumed Egavine really was in control here, and I could have handled *him.* I walked into a trap." She fished the shards of a smashed kwil needle out of her pocket, looked at them, and dropped them on the floor before her. "I got slammed around a little," she explained.

Calat laughed, said something in the Fleet tongue, grinning at her. She ignored him.

Egavine said, "My effects were secretly inspected while we were at the Fleet station, Dasinger, and the Fleetmen have been taking drugs to immunize themselves against my hypnotic agents. They disclosed this when Miss Mines brought the speedboat down. There was nothing I could do. I regret to say that they intend to murder us. They are waiting only to assure themselves that the star hyacinths actually are in the indicated compartment."

"Great!" Dasinger groaned. He put his hands back in a groping gesture to support himself on the bench.

"Still pretty feeble, I suppose?" Miss Mines inquired, gentle sympathy in her voice.

"I'm poisoned," he muttered brokenly. "The thing's left me paralyzed. . . ." He sagged sideways a little, his hand moving behind Duomart. He pinched her then in a markedly unparalyzed and vigorous manner.

Duomart's right eyelid flickered for an instant.

"Somebody wrung the little monster's neck before I got here," she remarked. "But there're other necks *I'd* sooner wring! Your partner's, for instance. Not that he's necessarily the biggest louse around at the moment." She nodded at Calat. "The two runches who call themselves Fleetmen don't intend to share the star hyacinths even with their own gang! They're rushing the job through so they can be on their way to the Hub before the Spy arrives. And don't think Liu Taunus trusts that muscle-bound foogal standing there, either! He's hanging on to the key of the Mooncat's console until he comes back up."

Calat smiled with a suggestion of strain, then said something in a flat, expressionless voice, staring at her.

"Oh, sure," she returned. "With Taunus holding me, I suppose?" She looked at Dasinger. "They're not shooting *me* right off, you know," she told him. "They're annoyed with me, so they're taking me along for something a little more special. But they'll have to skip the fun if the Spy shows up, or I'll be telling twenty armed Fleetmen exactly what kind of thieving cheats they have leading them!" She looked back at Calat, smiled, placed the tip of her tongue lightly between her lips for an instant, then pronounced a few dozen Fleet words in a clear, precise voice.

It must have been an extraordinarily un-flattering comment. Calat went white, then red. Half-smart tough had been Duomart's earlier description of him. It began to look like an accurate one...Dasinger felt a surge of pleased anticipation. His legs already were drawn well back beneath the bench; he shifted his weight slowly forwards now, keeping an expression of anxious concern on his face. Calat spoke in Fleetlingue again, voice thickening with rage.

Miss Mines replied sweetly, stood up. The challenge direct.

The Fleetman's face worked in incredu-lous fury. He shifted the gun to his left hand and came striding purposefully towards Miss

Mines, right fist cocked. Then, as Dasinger tensed his legs happily, a muffled thump from deep within the wreck announced the opening of the star hyacinth vault.

The sound was followed by instant proof that Hovig had trapped the vault.

Duomart and Calat screamed together. Dasinger drove himself forward off the bench, aiming for the Fleetman's legs, checked and turned for the gun which Calat, staggering and shrieking, his face distorted with lunatic terror, had flung aside. Dr. Egavine, alert for this contingency, already was stooping for the gun, hand outstretched, when Dasinger lunged against him, bowling him over.

*D*asinger came up with the gun, Quist pounding at his shoulders, flung the little man aside, turned back in a frenzy of urgency. Duomart twisted about on the floor near the far end of the compartment, arms covering her face. The noises that bubbled out from behind her arms set Dasinger's teeth on edge. She rolled over convulsively twice, stopped dangerously close to the edge of the jagged break in the deck, was turning again as Dasinger dropped beside her and caught her.

Immediately there was a heavy, painful blow on his shoulder. He glanced up, saw Quist running toward him, a rusted chunk of metal like the one he had thrown in his raised hand, and Egavine peering at both of them from the other side of the compartment. Dasinger flung a leg across Duomart, pinning her down, pulled out the gun, fired without aiming. Quist reversed his direction almost in mid-stride. Dasinger fired again, saw Egavine dart towards the lock, hesitate there an instant, then disappear down the ramp, Quist sprinting out frantically after him.

A moment later he drove one of the remaining kwil needles through the cloth of Duomart's uniform, and rammed the plunger down.

The drug hit hard and promptly. Between one instant and the next, the plunging and screaming ended; she drew in a long, shuddering breath, went limp, her eyes closing slowly. Dasinger was lifting her from the floor when the complete silence in the compartment caught his attention. He looked around. Calat was not in sight. And only then did he become aware of a familiar sensation . . . a Hovig generator's pulsing, savage storm of seeming nothingness, nullified by the drug in his blood.

He laid the unconscious girl on the bench, went on to the lock.

Dr. Egavine and Quist had vanished; the thick shrubbery along the lake bank stirred uneasily at twenty different points but he wasn't looking for the pair. With the Mooncat inaccessible to them, there was only one place they could go. Calat's body lay doubled up in the rocks below the ramp, almost sixty feet down, where other human bodies had lain six years earlier. Dasinger glanced over at the Fleet scout, went back into the compartment.

He was buckling himself into the third salvage suit when he heard the scout's lifeboat take off. At a guess Hovig's little private collection of star hyacinths was taking off with it. Dasinger decided he couldn't care less.

He snapped on the headpiece, then hesitated at the edge of the deck, looking down. A bubble of foggy white light was rising slowly through the water of the hold, and in a moment the headpiece of one of the other suits broke the oily surface, stayed there, bobbing gently about. Dasinger climbed down, brought Liu Taunus's body back up to the lock compartment, and recovered the Mooncat's master key.

He found Graylock floating in his suit against a bulkhead not far from the shattered vault where Hovig's two remaining generators thundered. Dasinger silenced the machines, fastened them and a small steel case containing nearly a hundred million credits' worth of star hyacinths to the salvage carrier, and towed it all up to the lock compartment.

A very few minutes later, the Mooncat lifted in somewhat jerky, erratic fashion from the planet's surface. As Dasinger had suspected, he lacked, and by a good deal, Miss Mines's trained sensitivity with the speedboat's controls; but he succeeded in wrestling the little ship up to a five-mile altitude where a subspace dive might be carried out in relative safety.

He was attempting then to get the Mooncat's nose turned away from the distant volcano ranges towards which she seemed determined to point when the detector needles slapped flat against their pins and the alarm bell sounded. A strange ship stood outlined in the Mooncat's stern screen.

*T*he image vanished as Dasinger hit the dive button, simultaneously flattening the speed controls with a slam of his hand. The semisolid subspace turbulence representing the mountain ranges beyond the lake flashed instantly past below him . . . within yards, it seemed. Another second put them beyond the planet's atmosphere. Then the Spy reappeared in subspace, following hard. A hammering series of explosions showed suddenly in the screens, kept up for a few hair-raising moments, began to drop back. Five minutes later, with the distance between them widening rapidly, the Spy gave up the chase, swung around and headed back towards the planet.

Dasinger shakily reduced his ship's speed to relatively sane level, kept her moving along another twenty minutes, then surfaced into normspace and set a general course for the Hub. He was a very fair yachtsman for a planeteer. But after riding the Mooncat for the short time he'd turned her loose to keep ahead of the Spy through the G2's stress zone, he didn't have to be told that in Fleet territory he was outclassed. He mopped his forehead, climbed gratefully out of the pilot seat and went to the cot he had hauled into the control room, to check on Duomart Mines.

She was still unconscious, of course; the dose he'd given her was enough to knock a kwil-sensitive out for at least a dozen hours. Dasinger looked down at the filth-smudged, pale face, the bruised cheeks and blackened left eye for a few seconds, then opened Dr. Egavine's medical kit to do what he could about getting Miss Mines patched up again.

Fifteen hours later she was still asleep, though to all outer appearances back in good repair. Dasinger happened to be bemusedly studying her face once more when she opened her eyes and gazed up at him.

"We made it! You . . ." She smiled, tried to sit up, looked startled, then indignant. "What's the idea of tying me down to this thing?"

Dasinger nodded. "I guess you're all there!" He reached down to unfasten her from the cot. "After what happened, I wasn't so sure you'd be entirely rational when the kwil wore off and you woke up."

Duomart paled a little. "I hadn't imagined . . ." She shook her blond head. "Well, let's skip that! I'll have nightmares for years. . . . What happened to the others?"

*D*asinger told her, concluded, "Egavine may have run into the Spy, but I doubt it. He'll probably show up in the Hub eventually with the gems he took from Calat, and if he doesn't get caught peddling them he may wind up with around a million credits . . . about the sixth part of what he would have collected if he'd stopped playing crooked and trying to get everything. I doubt the doctor will ever quit kicking himself for that!"

"Your agency gets the whole salvage fee now, eh?"

"Not exactly," Dasinger said. "Considering everything that's happened, the Kyth Interstellar Detective Agency would have to be extremely ungrateful if it didn't feel you'd earned

the same split we were going to give Dr. Egavine."

Miss Mines gazed at him in startled silence, flushed excitedly. "Think you can talk the
Kyth people into *that*, Dasinger?"

"I imagine so," Dasinger said, "since I
own the agency. That should finance your Willata Fleet operation very comfortably and still
leave a couple of million credits over for your
old age. I doubt we'll clear anything on Hovig's
generators. . . ."

Miss Mines looked uncomfortable. "Do
you have those things aboard?"

"At the moment. Disassembled of
course. Primarily I didn't want the Fleet gang to
get their hands on them. We might lose them in
space somewhere or take them back to the Federation for the scientists to poke over. We'll
discuss that on the way. Now, do you feel perky
enough to want a look at the stuff that's cost
around a hundred and fifty lives before it ever
hit the Hub's markets?"

"Couldn't feel perkier!" She straightened up expectantly. "Let's see them. . . ."

Dasinger turned away towards the wall where he had put down the little steel case with the loot of the Dosey Asteroids robbery.

Behind him, Duomart screamed.

He spun back to her, his face white. "What's the matter?"

Duomart was staring wide-eyed past him towards the instrument console, the back of one hand to her mouth. "That . . . the thing!"

"Thing?"

"Big . . . yellow . . . wet . . . *ugh!* It's ducked behind the console, Dasinger! It's lurking there!"

"Oh!" Dasinger said, relaxing. He smiled. "That's all right. Don't worry about it."

"Don't worry about . . . are you crazy?"

"Not in the least. I thought you were for a second, but it's very simple. You've worked off the kwil and now you're in the hangover period. You get hallucinations then, just as I usually do. For the next eight or nine hours, you'll be seeing odd things around from time to time. So what? They're not real."

"*A*ll right, they're not real, but they seem real enough while they're around," Duomart said. "I don't want to see them." She caught her breath and her hand flew up to her mouth again. "Dasinger, please, don't you have something that will put me back to sleep till I'm past the hangover too?"

Dasinger reflected. "One of Doc Egavine's hypno sprays will do it. I know enough of the mumbo jumbo to send you to dreamland for another ten hours." He smiled evilly. "Of course, you realize that means you're putting yourself completely in my power."

Duomart's eyes narrowed for an instant. She considered him, grinned. "I'll risk it," she said.

THE END